RESISTANCE FIGHTER

The Story of a Secret War

Dee Phillips

D1077530

READZONE

First published in this edition 2014

All rights reserved. No part of this publication may be reproduced, stored in a retrieval system, or transmitted, in any form, or by any means, electronic, mechanical, photocopying, or otherwise, without the prior permission of ReadZone Books Limited

© **Copyright Ruby Tuesday Books Limited 2014**
© **Copyright in this edition ReadZone Books 2014**

The right of the Author to be identified as the Author of this work has been asserted by the Author in accordance with the Copyright, Designs and Patents Act 1988

Every attempt has been made by the Publisher to secure appropriate permissions for material reproduced in this book. If there has been any oversight we will be happy to rectify the situation in future editions or reprints. Written submissions should be made to the Publishers.

British Library Cataloguing in Publication Data (CIP) is available for this title.

ISBN 978-1-78322-515-6

Printed in Malta by Melita Press

Developed and Created by Ruby Tuesday Books Ltd
Project Director – Ruth Owen
Designer – Elaine Wilkinson

Images courtesy of Alamy (cover, pages 1, 18, 19), Getty Images (pages 5, 8, 21, 30, 38b, 43), Public Domain (pages 10, 20, 38T) and Shutterstock.

Acknowledgements
With thanks to Lorraine Petersen, Educational Consultant, for her help in the development and creation of these books

Visit our website: www.readzonebooks.com

I carried messages for the Resistance.
Secret messages from fighter to fighter.
There were German soldiers everywhere.
I was always in danger.

RESISTANCE
FIGHTER

The Story of a Secret War

In World War II, Germany was at war with Britain and many other nations.

Germany invaded a number of countries including Poland, the Netherlands and France.

People in these countries lived under German occupation, or rule.

Thousands of people in occupied countries became resistance fighters.

They launched surprise attacks on German soldiers.

They blew up bridges and railways to make it hard for German forces to move around.

They spied on the Germans and sent information to Britain.

Britain helped the brave resistance fighters.

Secret agents were sent from Britain to occupied countries.

These highly trained men and women helped fight this secret war.

It's a cold autumn night.
Slowly, I shuffle along the street.
A young lad pushes past me.
He doesn't really see me.
I'm just an old woman.

The young lad looks a
little like Henri.

Henri my husband....

I met Henri in London.
He was French and very handsome.
The war had just begun.
We married after only a month.

Henri took me to live in France.
But then the Germans invaded.

"Go back to London," he said.
"I want you to be safe."
Then he went off to fight.

I was just 21 when I became a widow.
My heart was broken.

I worked as a nurse in London.
One day, a man came to the hospital.
"They tell me you speak French,
Betty," he said.
"Are you brave?"
"Will you help us to fight the Germans?"

Was I brave? I don't know.
My heart was broken.
I hated this war.
"Yes." I said. "I will help you."

I was sent for training.

I learned how to use a radio.
And how to send coded messages.

I learned how to jump from a plane.
And how to set up explosives.

I learned how to fire a gun.

And how to kill without making a sound.

It was a cold autumn night.
The night I went back to France.
I climbed into the plane.
I carried fake papers.
I carried a gun, and a small radio.

Was I brave? I don't know.
I hated this war.
I wanted to help.

CARTE D'IDENTITÉ

Nom **BOURDET**
Prénoms Sylvie Violette
Profession
Nationalité Française
Né le 9 août 1919
à Bergues - nord
Domicile

Empreintes Digitales

Signature du Titulaire,

We flew through the cold autumn night.
We flew into France.
The French Resistance lit the way for us.
I jumped from the plane.
Down, down towards
the lights.

I jumped from the plane as Betty, a nurse.
But I landed in France as Sylvie, a
secret agent.
A resistance fighter!

I carried secret messages for the Resistance.
I sent coded messages back to London.
There were German soldiers everywhere.
I was always in danger.

Was I brave? I don't know.
I hated this war.
My heart was broken.

19

One day I went to the town.
I had to meet another agent.
There were German soldiers
everywhere.
But I was just Sylvie.
A pretty French girl buying
bread and milk.

I sat outside a café.
A man sat down at my table.
I took a cigarette from my bag.
He lit my cigarette.
Then he walked away.

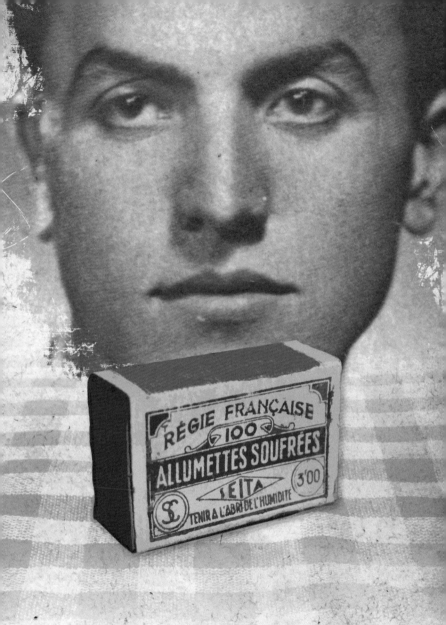

He left his matchbox on the table.

I picked up the matchbox.
I walked from the café.

A German soldier!
"What is your name?" he hissed.
"Show me your papers!"

Sweat trickled down my back.

"What is in the bag?"

I showed him…

Bread. Milk.

Money. Lipstick.

A handkerchief.

Cigarettes.

A matchbox.

Minutes passed.

He looked at my papers again.
Sweat trickled down my back.

He looked inside the packet
of cigarettes.

Then he turned away.
"On your way," he said.

The matchbox held a plan.
A plan to blow up a German
weapons factory.

Slowly, I shuffle into the shop.
I buy bread and milk.
A young girl serves me.
But she doesn't talk to me.
I'm just an old woman.

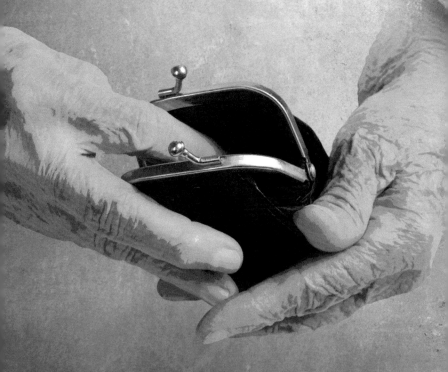

What interesting things could
I possibly have to say?

It was a cold autumn night.
The night we attacked
the factory.
We lay in the cold, wet grass.
We waited.

When the guards turned away, we ran. Ran through the darkness into the factory gate.

I set up the explosives.
I did what I had been trained to do.
Suddenly, I heard a noise.

"WHO'S THERE?"

said a German voice.

It was a young soldier.
I couldn't shoot him.
It would make too much noise.
I did what I had been trained to do.

My arm hit his chin.

HARD.

He fell to the ground.

DEAD.

We ran from the factory.
Back into the cold, autumn night.
Some German soldiers saw us.
Bullets tore into my leg.

I fell into the cold, wet grass.
But I shot back.
Again and again.

The other resistance fighters carried
me back to the dark forest.
The factory burned.
We had done what we had been
trained to do.

I shuffle slowly into
my house.
My leg still hurts on
these cold nights.

We destroyed that factory.

And many others.

We blew up bridges
and railways.
We killed many
soldiers.

I worked with the Resistance
until the end of the war.

I wasn't safe, Henri.

But I wanted to help.

I look in the mirror.
I think of the
lad on the street.
The girl in the shop.
What do they see?
Just an old woman.
But I see a girl who jumped
from a plane.
A girl who carried
a gun.
I still see Sylvie, the
resistance fighter.
The girl who fought
a secret war.

I smile at myself in the mirror.
Was I brave?
Perhaps I was.

RESISTANCE FIGHTER:
Behind the Story

Resistance fighters in occupied countries fought their secret war in many ways. Some groups carried out guerilla warfare. They attacked German convoys and sabotaged factories that made equipment for the Germans.

When British or American planes were shot down over occupied countries, the Resistance hid the airmen. Then they helped them escape back to Britain. Resistance groups helped Jews who were escaping from the Nazis.

Britain sent secret agents into occupied countries. These agents worked for the Special Operations Executive (SOE). SOE agents helped the Resistance fight back against the Germans. They arranged for weapons to be sent from Britain for the Resistance.

SOE agents and resistance groups spied on the Germans. Coded messages were sent back to Britain about German operations and plans. This helped the Allies make plans that would win the war.

Many SOE agents were secretly parachuted into France at night. Once there, they had to act like ordinary French people. Each agent had a false name and a cover story. Agents and resistance workers risked death to carry out their dangerous work.

The Final Resort

If an SOE agent or resistance fighter was captured, he or she might be interrogated by German soldiers or the Gestapo. The Gestapo were the German secret police. Torture would be used to make the agent give up information, such as plans that were underway or the names of other agents and resistance fighters. Then the agent might be killed. SOE agents carried a suicide pill. It was often hidden in a coat button. If captured, an agent could quickly end his or her life by swallowing the deadly pill.

French resistance fighters in the Alps in 1944

RESISTANCE FIGHTER –
What's next?

REAL
IDENTITY

Amanda Jones
15 years old
Born:
10/04/1999
London
Mother's Name:
Sue Jones

COVER
STORY

Imelda Swift
17 years old
Born:
04/10/1997
Manchester
Mother's Name:
Anna Swift

COVER STORY
WITH A PARTNER

Betty, the character in the story, pretended she was French and her name was Sylvie. Create a fake identity for yourself. Learn your new identity, then ask a friend to test you. Your friend should question you very fast, and try to catch you out. Remember – secret agents in WWII had to fool their German interrogators. The agents' lives depended on it!

Resistance workers and secret agents had to be creative to stay in touch with each other. On pages 22–23, Sylvie (Betty) receives a secret message hidden inside a matchbox. Imagine you have to pass a note to the person next to you. No one must suspect you. How would you do it?

REGIE FRANÇAISE
100
ALLUMETTES SOUFREES
LEITA
TENIR À L'ABRI DE L'HUMIDITE   3'00

The people Betty meets in the story do not realise she was once a resistance fighter. Many older people around you may have experienced exciting, dangerous or difficult times in their lives. Today, we talk openly about the things we do. We share experiences online. People from older generations, however, are more private about their lives.

Arrange to interview an older person. Ask that person to tell you about a memorable time in his or her life. He or she may even have memories of WWII. After the interview, discuss or think about these questions: Were you surprised by what you learned? Do you now see that person differently?

WAS I BRAVE?
IN A GROUP

Bravery can be shown in many ways. People sometimes surprise themselves by the things they can do. With your group, discuss bravery.

- How do you think it felt to be a secret agent or resistance fighter during WWII? What do you think made people risk their lives?

- In what ways do people show bravery today? What do you think motivates them?

- Can you think of a time when you were brave? Perhaps you stood up to a bully or needed to have treatment for a serious illness. What did that moment of personal bravery feel like? How did it change you afterwards?

45

Titles in the
Yesterday's Voices
series

We jump from our ship and attack. But something feels wrong. I know this place….

We face each other. Two proud samurai. Revenge burns in my heart.

We saw a treasure ship. Up went our black flag. They could not escape….

The work is so hard. I miss my home. Will my dream of America come true?

I jumped from the plane. I carried fake papers, a gun and a radio. Now I was Sylvie, a resistance fighter….

Every day we went on patrol. The Viet Cong hid in jungles and villages. We had to find them, before they found us.

GLADIATOR
The Story of a Fighter

I waited deep below the arena. Then it was my turn to fight. Kill or be killed!

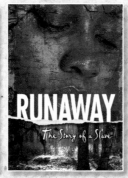

RUNAWAY
The Story of a Slave

I cannot live as a slave any longer. Tonight, I will escape and never go back.

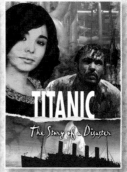

TITANIC
The Story of a Disaster

The ship is sinking into the icy sea. I don't want to die. Someone help us!

OVER THE TOP
The Story of a Soldier

I'm waiting in the trench. I am so afraid. Tomorrow we go over the top.

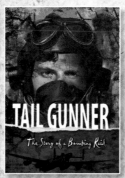

TAIL GUNNER
The Story of a Bombing Raid

Another night. Another bombing raid. Will this night be the one when we don't make it back?

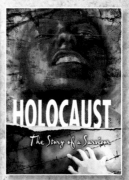

HOLOCAUST
The Story of a Survivor

They took my clothes and shaved my head. I was no longer a human.